TO Avery

Merry Christmas 2022

Rob Frith

Have a
Smile-o-licious day

Dedication

The most important thing to me is my children, my grandchildren and family.

This is dedicated to my daughter Samantha,
My sons Adam and Jason and my Grandchildren Jarett, Sawyer,
Alexis, Weston, Sullivan and Delaney (and soon baby Kristie).

THE DOLL-a magical Christmas is available as a two-act musical with seventeen songs.
Check it out on Facebook under The Doll- a magical Christmas

Edited by Karen A. Smith

The Doll
A Magical Christmas

by Rob Kristie

The Doll
A magical Christmas

CHAPTER ONE

The weather was mild for late December, but the steps were cold. Samantha adjusted the bottom of her coat so she could sit on it. Despite her blindness, she would often sit there alone listening to children talking, laughing and playing.

"Oh, look at that train set" said Jarett as he stared into the store window.

"Who cares about trains? Look at all those dolls and stuffed animals" said Alexis.

"Did you see the size of that one doll? She's as big as you are Alexis. In fact, she may be bigger" shouted Sullivan.

"Why do they call those jawbreakers…can they really break your jaw?" said Sawyer as he pointed to them through the candy store window.

The door to Samantha's house opens and her mother steps out.

"Sweetheart, do you want your scarf or hat before we head down to the church?"

"No Mom, it's not that cold out. What time does the choir practice begin?

"In about 10 minutes and I know how much you enjoy listening to them rehearse
 So, we better hurry."

Samantha's mother takes her by the hand, and they walk down the street together heading for the church.

Meanwhile, the new store owner Adam, steps out of his store to hang a "Grand Opening" sign.

"Hey mister, how much is that giant doll in the corner of the window," said Alexis.

"Why she's on sale today, in fact everything is on sale today," said Adam as he smiled.

.

"Do you have any Star Wars toys?" said Weston.

"Or any WrestleMania stuff?" asked Jarett

"I have all kinds of toys, books, jewelry, tools…Things for kids and things for adults. You name it and I probably have it," said the store owner.

A few shoppers start looking through the racks displayed outside and some go inside the store while the children continue window shopping.

Samantha and her mother return. "Samantha, I'm sorry we couldn't hear the choir today."

"Don't be sorry, Mommy. You had no way of knowing it was cancelled."

"Oh sweetie, that new store has opened. Mommy is just going to stop for a minute to look.".

Samantha's mom begins looking through one of the racks.

Adam walks up to Samantha,

"Good morning lil' lady, do you see anything you like? Is there anything I can show you?"

Samantha's mother runs to her daughter's side. "Sorry sir, she's my daughter and she is blind.".

"Oh I am so sorry young lady, I do apologize. I didn't realize you couldn't see."

"It's ok," said Samantha.

The store owner extends his hand to Samantha's mother. "I am Adam Barter and I am new here. This is the first day my store is open."

"I know, I watched you get your place ready. We live right next door here. My name is Ann and this is my daughter Samantha."

"I do feel bad about what I said Samantha. Ann, will you allow me to make it up to her?
 "That's not necessary Adam. It's fine, besides, we should be going."

"No please wait here one moment I'll be right back."

Adam rushes into his store and returns with the life-size doll.

"Here Samantha, I would like you to have this doll. Think of it as an early Christmas present," said Adam as he handed her the doll

Samantha reaches out and realizes that the doll is rather big.

"She's HUGE! ….and why is she so floppy?" as she shakes her.

Adam responds laughing, "She is rather large and she is floppy and that is because she's a ragdoll. She is made from old rags."

"Well thank you sir, is it OK Mom? Can I keep her?" said Samantha smiling.

"Yes, sweetheart, you can. What are you going to name her?" said Ann.

"I'm not sure. Maybe I'll name her after you mom. Or wait, she is so floppy maybe I'll just call her Flopsy. Yes, she is Flopsy! Oh, Thank you very much Mr. Barter.".

"Yes, thank you, Adam. That was very kind of you. Good luck with your store and Merry Christmas to you."

"It is my pleasure and Merry Christmas to both of you," replied Adam.

"Take my hand Samantha, I don't want you to fall,"

says Ann as they head into their house.

CHAPTER TWO

Samantha was sitting up in her bed, brushing her hair when her mother walked in carrying the doll.

"Where would you like me to put your doll Samantha?"

"Can she go in the rocking chair, Mom?"

"And then where am I supposed to sit when I read to you tonight?"

"I'm tired, Mom…I think I'm going to go right to sleep tonight if that's ok?"

"Sure Sweetheart, are you feeling alright?"

"Yeah" Samantha pauses and then says "Why don't the other kids ever ask me to play or talk to me Mommy? What's wrong with me?"

Ann hugs Samantha, "There is nothing wrong with you sweetheart, they are just afraid because they don't understand blindness."

"But why are they afraid? I'm the one who can't see. I'm the one who should be afraid, not them, they have their sight. Am I ugly Mommy?"

"NO, NO Samantha. You are a beautiful girl, in fact, you are very beautiful." Ann held back the tears and hugged her again. "You get some rest dear. We can talk about this more tomorrow, OK? Goodnight sweetheart".

"Goodnight Mommy"
Ann leaves and shuts off the overhead light, leaving the dim night light on even though Samantha doesn't need it.

She sits up in bed and reaches blindly for her new doll and pulls it close with a hug. "I wish I had a friend…..someone to talk to, laugh with and play with….. Will you be my friend Flopsy? Mom is great, but I need someone who is not an adult. Someone who I can share things with….someone I can….

Why am I talking to you?, she sighs, I need someone real….you're just a toy doll."
Samantha lies down and begins to sob as she tries to fall asleep. Eventually, she doze's off, and the doll falls to the floor.

"OUCH!" yelled a voice.

Startled and frightened, Samantha sits up in her bed and demands "Who said that? Who is in here? Mommy is that you?"

"HELLO-OOO!…. It's me, I'm down here…you know, the one you dropped on the Floor," said the voice.

"Oh, I must be dreaming. Wake up Samantha!" as she slaps her cheek lightly.

"No little girl, you are not dreaming" says the doll as she strolls across the room.

"Are you walking around the room? Could you just stay still for a moment?"

"I am walking around, but you can't see me can you?" said the doll

"Who's here really?......Mommy is that you?...it can't be the doll, Flopsy?…that can't be?" said Samantha in a puzzled voice.

"Flopsy? ….Please tell me you didn't name me Flopsy?
You couldn't think of anything better like, Gorgeous Joann or Princess Rebecca? I'm stuck with Flopsy?"

"Forget about the name, who are you really and how did you get in here?" cried Samantha.

Flopsy hits the light switch to illuminate the room and replies
"Well, I'm not really sure how I got here or where I am. I mean I can see that's it's a bedroom but…"

"Wait, you can see?" questioned Samantha.

"Of course I can see. I do have eyes silly," said Flopsy as she pointed to her eyes.

"I have eyes too, but I can't see…and I'm real, you're just a doll," said Samantha.

The doll walks back around the bed, crosses her arms and replies,
"Yeah but you're blind and I'm not….. So, what's your name?"

Samantha hesitates, "My name is Samantha. Why are you here?"

"I believe you requested a friend, did you not?"

"Yes, yes I did but how did you hear me? How can this be?" questioned Samantha.

"Hmmmmm ….maybe I'm not here at all and you are just dreaming. Maybe it's just your imagination taking over".
 Flopsy leans in and in a scary voice says, "Maybe I'm a ghost!"

"Oh stop! Why can't you give me a straight answer? I face enough scary things being blind.
 I don't need you to scare me too," cried Samantha.
 "Hey Sami sorry girlfriend, I'm just teasing. I'm just
being playful and having a little fun. I am your friend. I didn't mean to
upset you. Tell me about yourself. Tell me why you're looking for a new friend."

CHAPTER THREE

The next morning as Adam is opening his store for the day,
a police officer stops to introduce himself to the new store owner.

"Good morning sir, "said the officer.

Adam glances at the officers name tag, extends his hand and says, "Good
morning to you Officer Tustin, I'm Adam Barter."

"Nice to meet you Mr Barter and welcome to the neighborhood. You couldn't have
picked a finer part of town to start your business."

"Oh please, call me Adam and I'm sure you are right officer. Yesterday was
amazing. I met some of the locals and I got to open in time for Christmas." Adam said
with a hearty laugh.

"The decorations around town look fabulous, especially down Broad
Street. I see they are decorating a tree right here on our corner. Whose tree is it?"

"The tree belongs to the merchants on the block. They all participate in decorating
it….it's a community tree."
.

"Say officer, can you tell me anything about Ann and her daughter who live in the
house next door?" asked Adam.

"Oh you mean Mrs. Flannery?
I don't know them that well, I just know they were involved in an
automobile accident many years ago. Her husband died and the little girl was
blinded. Why do you ask?"

"Well, like I said, I met many of the local people yesterday, but those two really
captured my attention. Ann seemed like a wonderful woman and her daughter
Samantha was adorable," said Adam with a smile. "It's a pity about her blindness.
You say it was caused by the accident?"

"I believe so but I'm really not too sure. That's what I've been told but don't go by
me. I probably shouldn't have said anything."

"There she is now. Let me go talk to her. Thanks Officer Tustin".

"Well, I need to continue my rounds, Have a good day sir"

Adam walked toward Ann and smiles. "Hello Ann! How are you this beautiful day?"

"Good morning Adam". It is a beautiful day isn't it?
I want to thank you again for giving the doll to my daughter. That really made her happy and me too we both went home with a smile."

"Oh it was my pleasure. Samantha is a beautiful little girl. If you don't mind my asking, has she always been blind?"

"No said Ann, she was injured in an automobile accident when she was two years old. That's when I lost my husband, her father."

"I am so sorry," replied Adam, "It must be very difficult for both of you."

"Yes, especially around the holidays. I try to keep her busy and her mind off of the past but I also want her to know that he was a great man. It does get to be difficult at times. She gets lonely."

Adam frowns, "But there are lots of other children in the neighborhood."

"Unfortunately, the other kids in the neighborhood don't pay any attention to her. That's why when you talked to her and gave her that gift it really made her day."

"I'm glad that made both of you happy. That completed my day and I always say, any completed day is a good day."

"Well Adam I must get going. Have a great day and maybe Samantha and I will stop in the store later this afternoon," said Ann.

"Sounds wonderful…Oh yeah, the store…. I almost forgot. I have to open up, see you later." as he hurries to unlock the door.

CHAPTER FOUR

Samantha sat up in her bed.

"Wow, what a dream!" she stretches and runs her fingers through her hair.

A voice comes from the other side of the room.

"Cool, you had a dream, what was it about?" Something bumps against her bed.

"No, this cannot be. Am I still asleep and still dreaming?"

"We are not going to go through this again are we Sami whammy?" replied Flopsy.

"My name is NOT Sami Whammy…it's Samantha! How can this be happening?
I'm so confused.
Ok, if you are really here, what did we talk about last night?"

Samantha hears soft footsteps move from one side to the other side of the bed where she is facing.
"We talked about using your imagination. We talked about flying and we
talked about playing with these toys that look like they have never been touched.
and what it would be like if…."

Samantha folds her arms across her chest "I play with my toys….. sometimes"

"Oh stop, you do not. These toys are not played with. They are perfectly placed and
way too neat. It looks more like a display in a museum. I just want to pull them all down
and toss them around."

"Oh please don't, I'll be tripping over them," cried Samantha.

"Oh the poor little blind girl," said Flopsy as she covered her mouth and makes
sounds like Darth Vader. "Use the force Samantha. Let the force be with you."

Shaking her head, a puzzled Samantha says, "What are you doing? What was that
supposed to be?"

"Hmmmm, you probably didn't see that movie, huh? I mean, you being blind and all. Just forget I mentioned it, really."

"And how do you know about a movie? How do you know about anything? You are not real, you're just a doll!" yelled Samantha.

"So, I suppose I can't talk either …or sing or dance or play…but like I already said, you don't play in here either."

Samantha lowers her head and says, "It's not much fun playing all by yourself."
She looks in the direction of Floppy's voice,
"Will you play with me Flopsy? Will you teach me how to use my imagination? I really don't know how."

Flopsy grabs Samantha's hand and says "Yes I'll teach you and you will experience a whole new world of creativity and wonders.
I want you to learn and remember this little poem ok?.....

If you can Imagine
You can create
You can do anything
Don't let your dreams wait.
Dreams have no boundaries,
No rules that apply.
You can do anything
If only you try."

"That's really pretty. I'm not sure I understand what it all means but I am willing to try," said Samantha.
"Good because we are going to get started right away. Come on now, get up and get dressed, we're going to the playground!" exclaimed Flopsy.

"What?...NO WAY!. I can't go to the playground, that's across the street and that is far too dangerous. And why do we need to go there?" said Samantha.

"Silly Dilly…because with a little help from me, a swing, and your imagination, I am going to teach you what it is like to fly. Did you forget already what we talked about last night and how riding a bike or swinging on a swing makes it feel like you're flying?" said Flopsy.

"No, I remember but you never mentioned going over to the playground." Samantha shakes her head and waves her hands indicating NO!.

Flopsy says "HELLO!... bike riding is a little too dangerous for a blind girl… but a swing we can do... There is no danger with a swing and its right across the street so get dressed Helen Keller."

"Hey! I know who Helen Keller is, stop making fun of me."

"How do you know Helen Keller and not know Darth Vadar? We need to work on your priorities, girlfriend." as she laughs out loud.

"My mother read the book about Helen Keller to me. Why are you being so mean to me? I thought you wanted to be my friend," said Samantha.

Flopsy pauses and says,
"You're right Samantha. I am sorry, I'm just trying to motivate you. I'm trying to get you excited about venturing into a new world of creativity and using your imagination, that's all.
So, let's get you dressed. I have a feeling this is going to be a smile-o-licious day."

"Smile- what?"

"Smile-o-licious!" said Flopsy

"That is not a real word. It's something you made up." responded Samantha.

Flopsy smiled and replied, "You're right, it is something I made up, but it is a word. I said it, you heard it, and we both understood it so that makes it a real word."

"But I didn't understand it, what does it mean?" Shaking her head in doubt.

"Oh dear…it means, it's so good it makes you want to smile. Now get dressed, we're about to start your flying lesson….But wait, first come here and give me your hand." said Flopsy.

Flopsy leads Samantha over to the easel chalk board standing in her room.

"I'm not sure why a blind girl has a chalk board in her room but I'm sure there's a good reason. Do you know how to write?"

"No, I don't" said Samantha "And yes, there is a good reason. My Grandmother who lives in Connecticut sent it to me as a gift. She's senile, which means she forgets a lot of things and doesn't always think right."

"Right, I know what it means. Let's move on. Give me your hand Samantha".
Flopsy grabs a piece of chalk, grabs and moves Samantha's hand helping her write on the chalkboard.
Together they write the number 2, the number 4 and a question mark on the chalk board.

"What did we draw?" said Samantha. "
We didn't draw anything we wrote the number 2, the number 4 and a question mark," said Flopsy

"Why, what does that mean?"
Flopsy takes both of Samantha's hands, holds them and says "It's my pledge to you Samantha. We'll be 2- together, 4- forever, ?. whatever.
That's how long we will be friends regardless what happens"

Samantha smiles and she was pretty sure Flopsy was smiling with her.

CHAPTER FIVE

"Oh Nancy isn't it wonderful? I love this time of year. Look at the smiles on the children's faces" said Thelma
"I love seeing them playing, I love the Christmas Decorations, the music and Look, they've started to decorate the community tree."

"These kids are too noisy, and did you see the prices of a real tree this year? Its outrageous. I can't wait till it's all over. I agree with Scrooge, Bah Humbug!" Said Nancy. .

"You are such an old fart" said Thelma. "You need to lighten up and enjoy the season. Think about your children and grandchildren. Now not another word from you unless its's attached to a smile."

"Good Morning ladies how are you today?" said Adam.

"Oh we're just Peachy and Happy happy happy," said Nancy with a bit of sarcasm.

"Don't pay any attention to her, she's an old grouch.
Your store looks busy today, Adam," said Thelma.

"Yes. I got in some new Christmas lights and some great holiday cake pans. You should come inside and see what I have," said Adam with a huge smile.

The ladies and Adam walked into his store followed by the children who had been peering through the windows.

Flopsy cracks open the door of Samantha's house and looks around. "The coast is clear. Come on." She tugs gently on Samantha's arm. She really wants Samantha to do it on her own.

"You're a slooow poooke. Come on, hurry up."
"I'm scared, are you sure this is safe? We have to get back quickly before my mother finds out. If I get caught I will be in big trouble and Santa won't bring me any gifts for Christmas," cried Samantha.

"Oh right, you find it hard to believe in me but Santa's not a problem? You are unbelievable.
Now come on, there no traffic.

Let's cross the street to the playground," said Flopsy.

"Are you sure there's no traffic? I hear something," said a frightened Samantha.

"Well of course **you do** …why does that not surprise me? Oh and there is no one at the playground hurry, we'll have it all to ourselves," shouted Flopsy.

Flopsy grabs Samantha's hand and the two dash across the street.
A few moments later, Thelma and Nancy come out of the store and return to the bus stop to wait for the bus.

"He really does have some great deals in his store," said Nancy.

"Yeah and it was nice of him to hold our packages for us until we get back this way we don't have to carry them all around the city," said Thelma as she glances in the direction of the playground. "Say, isn't that the little blind girl over there in the playground?"

Nancy glances up and says "Yeah I think it is, so what, can't her mother take her over to the playground?"

"Well yeah, she can, but she wouldn't leave her over there on her own would she? Wait, there is someone else sitting under the tree, another one of the kids maybe? I don't know it's hard to tell but she is swinging really high."
Nancy looks over again and says "I'm sure her mother took her over with another one of the neighborhood kids. She's probably coming right back or is somewhere close by. But you're right Thelma, she is swinging pretty high on that swing."

Both women gasp as Thelma shouts, "OH MY, she fell off the swing. She hit the ground hard and she is not moving. Someone call 9-1-1!"
Hearing the shouting, Adam and all the children rush out from the store and hurry to the corner where the ladies are shouting.

"CALL 911, THAT LITTLE GIRL IS NOT MOVING, HURRY!"
Adam using his cell phone calls Emergency services as the kids and two ladies run across the street to the little girl Samantha.

CHAPTER SIX

"What is taking so long?" said Ann as she paced back and forth.

"I'm sure the doctor will be here any minute Ann. Why don't you sit down?" said Adam as he stepped toward her.

"Look at her…. she is lying there lifeless with monitors beeping and tubes running to her arm."

"Here comes the doctor now Ann."

"What is wrong with my little girl Doctor? She's going to be alright, isn't she?" said Ann in a quivering voice.

"I'm not certain yet. We are conducting some tests and I should have the results very soon. You say she fell off a swing?" questioned the Doctor.

"Yes! I don't know what she was doing over the playground all alone or how she even got there but, some of the neighbors saw her fall off the swing and hit her head.
Please say she's going to be OK Doctor?" Tears fall from her eyes.

Adam rushed to Ann's side and held her gently.

"She's going to be all right Ann. She's in good hands and they will do everything they can to help her. Right Doctor?"

"Yes of course. I will be back shortly." The doctor placed the chart back on Samantha's hospital bed and left the room.

"Adam, how did my little angel get to that playground, and why was she over there?" sobbed Ann as she stared out the window in the direction of the playground.

"I don't know Ann, maybe one of the neighborhood kids took her there. Does she have a habit of wandering on her own? Do you take her to the playground frequently?"

"No Adam, we have only gone there a few times and it's not like her to attempt anything like that. Samantha is a very frightened and clingy child. She would never venture anywhere without me….never!"

"Well then it must have been one of the local kids. I believe the police were questioning all of them from the neighborhood. Apparently, some were at the corner helping decorate the town Christmas tree just before it happened," replied Adam.

"Oh my, that's right, Christmas is only 2 days away. She must be better by Christmas, she must.

Ann goes to her daughter's bedside, pulls a chair closer and sits down grasping her daughter's hand. Adam grabs his coat and turns to Ann.

"I'm sure she will be fine soon Ann, very soon. I need to leave now and get back to my store for a little while. Is there anything I can bring you? Maybe something to eat or drink?"

Ann doesn't look up and silently stares at her daughter, while holding her hand and stroking her hair. She lowers her head and says,

"Dear God, please help my baby girl. It isn't her time yet, it can't be. Please don't take away our time. Please God."

CHAPTER SEVEN

It's Christmas Eve the neighborhood children and some of the adults were outside still hanging ornaments on the community tree when Adam approached.

"Good evening ladies, and Merry Christmas to you," said Adam.

"Same to you, kind sir," responds Nancy.

"How is Ann? Any update on little Samantha?" said Thelma.

"The doctor said that her vitals have improved but she is still in a coma. Ann is drained. I feel so bad for her. She never wants to leave the hospital. She insisted that I not come there tonight. She wants to be alone with her daughter on Christmas Eve."

"That is so sad. Tell her that Nancy and Thelma are praying for her and Samantha."

The neighborhood kids run over to talk Adam.

"How is Samantha?" said one little girl, "Is she doing better?" said another. "Will she make it home in time for Christmas?" asked one of the boys.

"No kids, it doesn't look like that will happen. She is still in a coma."

"She's missing all the colorful lights and decorations and she's going to miss Santa," said lil' five-year-old Rosemary.

"Oh Rosemary, she's blind, she can't see anything, you goofy girl," said one of the boys.

"She's too young to understand that young man," scolded Thelma.

"We want to wish her a Merry Christmas so maybe we can make a Christmas card for her. Will you take it to her for us, mister?" said Alexis.

"I would be delighted to deliver it for you. I will take it to her tomorrow, Christmas day Is that ok with you kids?"

"Yes and thank you, mister." responded one little girl and they all smiled.

Another gentleman from the neighborhood approached Adam and asks about the little girl and her mother.

"This is a good thing, the entire neighborhood is concerned about them," said Adam.

"Oh, everyone has been asking about them. I think we should get a fruit basket or something," said Thelma.

"For where, the hospital or the house?…And only the mother can enjoy that since the little girl is in a coma," replied Nancy.

"Perhaps you're right Nancy but I just feel like we should do something. The kids had a great idea with making their own card, what can we do?" said Thelma as she pondered a few minutes.

"Well I have to run over to the church and pick up Samantha's rag doll that I gave her. The ladies church auxiliary is cleaning it up and replacing the eyes. It got damaged over at the playground," said Adam

All of a sudden, Thelma's eyes got big, she turned to Nancy and Adam smiled, and said, "I have a great idea. They both love to go listen to the church choir rehearse so maybe we can get the choir to go to the Hospital and sing."

"That is a wonderful idea, good thinking," said Adam.

"Well you gave me the idea when you mentioned the doll being at the church. Do you think the hospital will allow it?" questioned Thelma.

"I don't see why not. If they don't, we'll sing," Nancy said with pride.

"Oh please, this is supposed to be a good thing, not torture," said Thelma.

They all chuckled.

"Now I want to do something too." said Adam. "Maybe I can sneak a gift into the hospital for Ann and maybe take Samantha her doll. That sounds good?"

"Yeah it does," said the ladies.

CHAPTER EIGHT

As the doctor swings open the door to Samantha's room, he sees that Ann is sound asleep in the large cushy chair.

Quietly he glances at the medical chart and makes a note.
As he places the chart back on the bed he whispers to Samantha…"Merry Christmas, lil one."

He turns and sees the doll sitting on the floor and a present sitting on the table next to Ann's chair.
He smiles and silently moves his lips to say "Merry Christmas" to Ann as he leaves.

Soon afterwards, Ann stretches and yawns but does not notice the doll or her gift.
She gets up and walks over to Samantha. She brushes her daughter's hair back with her hand and kisses her forehead.

"Merry Christmas sweetheart. I love you." She pauses "Mommy will be right back, I need to use the little girl's room." With that, Ann leaves the room.

"YOO HOO Hey sleepy head…get up!" Flopsy says as she rises and begins walking around the room.

"You do know it's Christmas right Sammy Whammy? ….Oh that's right, you don't like that name do you?, sorry SAMANTHA….NOW GET UP!"
Samantha does not move.

"Looks like Mom got a present. I bet it's from the store owner. I think he is kind of sweet on your mom don't you agree, Samantha?"

No response…..

"Well if you're not going to wake up, I'm going to go exploring." said Flopsy and with that she ventured out of Samantha's room.

Moments later Ann walks back into the room and notices the beautifully wrapped gift sitting on the table next to a vase of flowers. She smiles because she knows the flowers are from Adam and she sees that the gift is labeled to her.

Just then Adam walks into the room and says, "Good Morning Ann and Merry Christmas to you."

"Merry Christmas to you too Adam, and thank you for my gift. I'm afraid I didn't get to purchase any gifts for anyone this year," said Ann as she shakes her head and looks down at the floor.
"And I see you brought Samantha flowers again. That is very thoughtful of you, thank you."

"I know she can't see them", said Adam, "but I get the ones that smell the best. When she wakes up I know she will smell them. By the way Nancy, Thelma and just about everyone in the neighborhood sends their thoughts and prayers as well as Christmas wishes for both you and Samantha….."

Adam peers around the room. "Where did the doll go?"

"The Doll? ….the rag doll that you gave her? You brought that here too?" said Ann.

"Yeah, the folks from the church repaired the broken eyes and cleaned it up. I set it right there on the floor," said Adam in a puzzled tone.

Right then, the Doctor walks into Samantha's room with another little girl who is wearing a cast and dragging the Doll. The Doctor looks across the room to where he had seen the doll sitting on the floor earlier and sees that it is no longer there.

I found this little girl, who is another patient on this floor, playing with this doll. I knew I had seen it in this room so I brought her back here with it. It was here earlier wasn't it?" said the Doctor.

"Yes," said Adam, "It belongs to Samantha here."

Ann walks over to the little girl and says with a smile "I'm sure you just wanted to play with the Doll right little one?...what is your name?"

"She doesn't speak. She hasn't said a word since they brought her in. She was the only survivor of an automobile crash. One of those senseless texting accidents," said the Doctor.

"Oh my, that is awful …she lost her parents?...they were texting?" asks Ann.

"No, she is an orphan. She was with two care providers who were driving her to the Philadelphia Orphanage.
It was the other driver, a young teen boy who was texting. He didn't survive either."

The doctor motions to the little girl "Give this lady the Doll, it belongs to her daughter."

With a sad face the little girl lets go of the Doll. It drops to the floor and as she runs out of the room, she bumps into a nurse coming in.

"I'm certain she just wandered in the room, saw the doll and wanted to play with it for a while," said the Doctor.

"That lil girl was in here again?" questioned the nurse.

"Again? What do you mean?" asked Ann.

As the nurse walked over to check on Samantha she replied, "The other night when I was working the night shift, I found her in here staring at your daughter. You were sound asleep in the chair and I didn't want to disturb you. I just took her by the hand and led her back to her room. Doctor, that's the little girl who hasn't said a word since she was admitted."

"Yes I recall, thank you nurse. I'm sure it was all harmless. Well I must
 continue with my rounds. Merry Christmas everyone."

"Merry Christmas Doctor and thank you" said Ann and Adam.

CHAPTER NINE

Adam is standing outside his store with his arms crossed, looking up and down the street as Nancy and Thelma approach.

"What's wrong Mr. Barter? You don't look too happy," said Thelma.

"I'm not" he replied. "Look at these people. They are like zombies. It's only three days after Christmas and all of a sudden, all the love, happiness and joy is gone. They have all fallen back into their humdrum lives. I don't get it.
Not one person has asked about Ann or Samantha in two days."

"Well that's why we walked over to talk to you. We wanted to ask how they were doing and we have something to tell you," said Thelma.

"Not much of a change I'm afraid. The doctor did say her vital signs have improved but she is still in a coma. Ann is hanging in there but she is exhausted and very depressed."

"I'm sure she is," replied Nancy.

"Well we have some good news" said Thelma.
"Remember we were trying to get the church choir over to the hospital to sing but they couldn't because of church services and other engagements they had? Well they can go there tomorrow. They are going to sing some Christmas carols for little Samantha."

"That is awesome, Ann will love that. Should I tell her or do you want it to be a surprise?" asked Adam

"Let's surprise her. We've already asked the hospital if it would be OK and they said yes as long as it's not too many people and we're not there too long," said Thelma smiling.

Just then a few of the kids from the neighborhood approached and all started talking at the same time.
"How is Samantha?"?asked Jarett.

"Is she getting any better?" asked Alexis.

"Did Santa come visit her in the hospital?" shouted Weston.

"No children. She is not any better and she doesn't even know that Christmas has come and gone," said Adam sadly.

"See, the children still care, Bless their souls. Hey kids, we are going to have the choir from church go there tomorrow and sing carols for her," said Thelma.

"Can we go too?" asked Sawyer.

"Yeah can we go?" yelled all the children.

"No I'm afraid the hospital will only allow so many visitors but thank you," said Adam.

"That's not fair," said Rosemary "We want to go too!"

One of the older kids motioned for all the children to follow him. Once they were far enough away from the store owner and ladies he said.

"I have an idea."

All the children smiled as they listened to his plan.

CHAPTER TEN

"Is the cafeteria still open?" said Ann to the nurse.

"No sorry, it closed about a half hour ago.

"Well looks like another vending machine night for me huh?" said Ann.

"Why don't you go to the nurses' lounge? We still have all this food left over that patients brought in for the holidays. Make yourself a sandwich, plus there is candy and fruit. There's plenty. So please, go help yourself," insisted the nurse.

"Why thank you. You're sure it's ok?" questioned Ann.

"Sure! Come with me I'll show you where everything is, and I just might join you," said the nurse as she laughed.

As they left the room, they shut the door behind them.

"OK …enough is enough" shouted Flopsy as she stood up and walked to Samantha's bed.

"You need to get your act together girlfriend. We have been here too long. You have had plenty of rest and we are missing out on way too much adventurous playtime, so get up."

"Did you hear me Samantha?"

No response

"OK ….. be that way. I know what I need to do here. I'm going to go and get some help. I'll be right back…don't go anywhere". Flopsy left the room.

A few minutes later the little girl with the cast returns with the Doll.

"Hello?" said the little girl. "Are you asleep?"

"Are you still alive?"

"My name is Ann Marie…. And I want to know, how did you get my doll? And why won't you wake up?"

The door opens slowly, and it is Ann, Samantha's mother. She hears the little girl talking.

"Hello again, sweetheart. So, you CAN talk. I just heard you talking to my daughter."

"Yes, but how come she doesn't talk, why doesn't she answer me?" said the little girl.

"She is in a coma. It's like a very deep sleep and she can't hear anything," said Ann. "What is your name?"

"I'm Ann Marie. Why did she turn into a coma?"

Ann smiles and replies, "She didn't turn into one, she had an accident…a bad fall. She hit her head very hard and it put her into this deep sleep. Did you come to play with her doll again?"

"It's not her doll, its mine," said Ann Marie.

"What makes you think it's your doll sweetheart?" said Ann

"Because when I woke up it was in my room, I didn't come take it. And even though it does have different eyes, it looks like my doll that I lost. Plus, my initials should be on the tickler" said Ann Marie.

"The tickler? What is that?" said Ann smiling.

"You know, the label in the collar…it always tickles the back of my neck, so I call it the tickler. My initials AM are written right there, see" said Ann Marie as she shows the tag to Ann.

With a curious smile Ann says, "How do I know you didn't put your initials there just now?"

"Because I'm left-handed and my arm and wrist are broken… see?" as she lifts up her arm in the cast. "Besides, why would I lie about it? Just the eyes, they are different," said Ann Marie.

"Well Flopsy did have different eyes but they got damaged, so I removed them and I sewed buttons on as eyes."

"Oh…..OK. I lost it last week when I was in a car accident. But I will let Samantha play with my doll if she wakes up. We can share her. ….Who's Flopsy?"

"That is very sweet of you Ann Marie, Samantha would like that…..Samantha would like you. Oh and Flopsy is what my daughter named the doll," said Ann.

"Flopsy…, its cute. OK I got to go but I will leave the doll here for Samantha when she wakes up.

Bye Samantha, bye Samantha's mom, bye Flopsy." Ann Marie giggled and left the room.

CHAPTER ELEVEN

"SILENT NIGHT, HOLY NIGHT. ALL IS CALM, ALL IS BRIGHT…" The beautiful voices of the choir rang out down the hallway of the hospital.

"Oh, I hope my daughter can hear them. It so wonderful of the choir to come here and sing for her,"

"It was Thelma and Nancy's idea. They went and asked them to come sing for Samantha and then afterwards, they will also go visit other floors of the hospital," said Adam.

"We were hoping that maybe the singing would help but it doesn't appear that it has," said Thelma

"It's helping me," said Ann "I am very grateful. Now I feel like today is Christmas."

A teenage boy enters the room "Excuse me, your Samantha's mom right?"

"Yes I am," replied Ann

"Well me and some of the other kids from the neighborhood were wondering, what are Samantha's favorite Christmas songs?"

"Hmmm, she likes Rudolph the Red-nosed Reindeer, but she also loved that one by the Chipmunks, whatever it's called. Why do you ask young man?"

"You'll see, …..can that window open?" asked the teenager.

"It does a little but not much said Adam…there, I opened it as far as it will go"

"OK thank you" With that the boy ran out of the room.

The doctor entered Samantha's room and proceeded to examine her. "Hello, Mrs. Flannery, I see our patient has some very talented visitors today. Thanks for stopping by and entertaining us."

"By the way Mrs Flannery, you're right, that little girl down the hall is talking now. That's a good thing.".

"Yes, she talked up a storm while she was here. Oh look here she is now. Hello Ann Marie."

"Hello, did Samantha wake up yet? I'm sure she did with all this singing."

"No I'm afraid she hasn't yet. I see you brought the doll with you."

"Why does this little girl have Samantha's doll?" asked Adam.

"It was her doll to begin with, Adam. Apparently she lost it when she was in a car accident,"

"Well I did find it on the side of the road. I cleaned it up and brought it to my store to sell. I always say, one man's trash is another man's treasure." as he smiled.

"Ann Marie was telling me the story about how she lost her doll, I just didn't get the chance to tell you about…."

Just then, Ann was interrupted by more voices. These voices were coming from outside the hospital. It was all the kids from the neighborhood and some of the grown-ups, too. They were all standing on the hill singing.

"*RUDOLPH THE RED-NOSED REINDEER HAD A VERY SHINY NOSE….*"
Everyone was singing at the top of their lungs….
"All of the other reindeer used to laugh and call him names. They never let poor Rudolph, play in any reindeer games."

"I never thought about it but Samantha was like Rudolph, The other kids never asked her to Play," said Ann.

"She's not alone today," said Adam

"No, she is not" replied Ann with a smile.

Little Ann Marie puts Flopsy on the bed with Samantha and walks over to the window with the others to look at the crowd on the hill and listen to them sing.

The doll starts to fall off the bed but is grabbed by a hand.
 It is Samantha's hand that catches her. The doctor and nurse stare in amazement.

"Hurry, she is becoming responsive," yelled the doctor

Ann spins around and sees her daughter slowing sitting up as she clings to the doll.

"Samantha? Sweetheart!" cries Ann as she runs to her daughter's side.
She wraps her arms around her tightly and they both begin to cry.

"Mommy, oh Mommy….where were you?" cried Samantha. "I looked
everywhere for you but couldn't find you. I heard singing but I couldn't tell
where it was coming from. If it wasn't for Flopsy taking my hand and leading
me here, I never would have found…" Samantha pauses begins to shake and covers
her eyes.

"What's wrong Samantha?...doctor help her" screamed Ann

The doctor removes her hands from her face and head and asks "What's wrong
Samantha do you have pain? Is your head hurting you?"

"No it's not….. I don't know what it is I don't know how to describe it, but it hurts,
….it's …it's bright?"
The doctor shines a light in Samantha's eye with no reaction but when he shines
it in the other eyes she quickly covers her face and turns away.

"What is wrong doctor? Am I going crazy or did she just react to your light?"
questioned Ann.
Everybody in the room gathers around Samantha's bed. The kids outside are still
singing with no idea what's going on.

"Yes she did. I need everyone to leave the room," replied the doctor.

"I can't leave," cried Ann

"Nurse! I want EVERYONE out immediately!" yelled the Doctor.

CHAPTER TWELVE

Ann paces back and forth in the hallway, while Adam and the others try to comfort her.

"I'm going back in. I need to see my daughter," cries Ann.

"The doctor is taking care of her Ann. Please calm down, I'm sure everything is fine and he is doing all he can for her," said Adam, in a reassuring voice.

Just then the doctor opens the door and walks out of the room. Ann runs up to him,

"How is Samantha? Is she ok doctor?."

"Tell me, did she ever complain about headaches?" asked the doctor.

"No, not really, well maybe occasionally but nothing that seemed out of the ordinary. Why do you ask?"

"Do you know what the Carotid artery is?" asked the doctor.

"No doctor, please speak English to me because I don't understand," said Ann.

"Well this artery controls blood flow to the brain and sometimes it can have a blockage that interferes with a person's sight. A hard impact or fall along with certain medicines that thin the blood can remove a blockage," explained the doctor.

"Meaning what?...Is my daughter in some other danger? I need to see her doctor….I need to see her now!" demanded Ann.

"Funny you should say that, I think she wants to see you too. In fact, I know she is anxious to see her mother," said the doctor with a huge smile.

"See me? What do you mean see me?" Ann said in a puzzling voice as she hurried into Samantha's room.

There was Samantha, sitting up in bed looking at her doll Flopsy. She quickly turned as her mother burst into the room.

"Mommy? Mommy is that you? It is you isn't it?

I can see you, Mom, I can see everything!"
cried Samantha.

"Oh Sweetheart you can see? You're alright?" said her mom in an excited voice.

"I can see out of one eye, Mom. The doctor said maybe the other one will clear later
 but I can see you, Samantha pauses and smiles. "You are so beautiful mommy…I love you."

They are holding each other crying with happiness as the others all entered the room.

"Hello Samantha, I'm Adam."

"And we're Nancy and Thelma from the neighborhood" We're all so happy for you
my child," said Nancy

"And who are you?" asked Samantha to the little girl in the cast.

"I'm Ann Marie. It's about time you woke up. We have been waiting for you,"
said Ann Marie, holding up the doll.

"We? You mean you and, wait, is that my doll Flopsy?" asked Samantha.

"Yeah, me and Flopsy.
By the way, I really do like the name Flopsy, She doesn't, but she
doesn't get to name herself does she?...we didn't"

Both little girls laugh and suddenly Samantha stops and says,
"Who is that singing? They're singing one of my favorites. The Chipmunks
"Christmas Don't Be Late."

"Look out the window." said her mom, "It's the kids from the neighborhood. They
 are here singing for you, Sweetheart."

Samantha walks to the window with her mother, Adam and Ann
Marie by her side. As she looks out the window the children all stop singing and
cheer and clap with excitement.

"MERRY CHRISTMAS Samantha, Welcome back!" yelled the kids.

"Wait, that's right Christmas…. today is Christmas or I missed it?" questioned Samantha.

Ann starts to tell her that Christmas has passed but Adam jumps in and says
"Yes Samantha, you did not miss Christmas. Today is Christmas."

Ann hesitates but then says, "Yes", "Today is Christmas! Merry Christmas sweetheart!"

"From now on every day is Christmas, just because we said so. Besides, every day should be like Christmas," said Adam with a hearty laugh.

"Wow, Imagine that, everyday will be Christmas." said Ann Marie. "That will make every day A smile-a-licious day,"

"Did you just say smile-a-licious" Where did you get that word from?"
questioned Samantha.

"I don't know," said Ann Marie "it just came out.".
Both girls turn and look at the doll that is propped up on the bed.

"What is wrong with her one eye?" said Ann Marie.

What do you mean? Does she look different? This is the first time I'm seeing her
said Samantha.

"Oh, it looks like one of her eyes fell off again…just the piece of thread is hanging there. I can
 sew it back on," said Ann.

"NO don't, it looks cool" said Ann Marie. "Kinda looks like she is winking"

"I like it too Mommy let's leave her that way!" said Samantha

Adam walks over to Ann and says "Looks creepy to me"

"Yeah" said Ann, "it is a little creepy but it does look like she is winking.
And her smile, It's different, isn't it?"

"I don't know, maybe, but how? Let's just get you and your daughter back home" said Adam.

"And you know what Adam, it's kind of funny. Now my daughter can see out of one eye and
the Doll only has one eye." This is strange Adam…very strange!"

Holding Flopsy, Samantha joins Ann Marie at the window looking out and waving to the kids.

Samantha looks at the doll and then at Ann Marie and says,

"I do have a question about Flopsy"

"Sure, what is it?"

"Did she ever…….well, did she ever….talk, to you?"

"Shhh" said Ann Marie with a smile.

They both giggled..

The End

**"Silent night" was written by
Franz Xaver Gruber to lyrics by Joseph Mohr**

**"Christmas don't be late" was written by
: Ross Bagdasarian Sr.**

<u>**THE DOLL-a magical Christmas**</u> is available as a two act musical
with seventeen songs. Check it out on Facebook under
The Doll- a magical Christmas

Illustration by Lauren Farrar

Made in the USA
Monee, IL
13 October 2020